First published by Parragon in 2009

Parragon
Queen Street House
4 Queen Street
Bath BA1 1HE, UK

ISBN 978-1-4075-8884-1

Printed in China

Jungle Tales

Bath New York Singapore Hong Kong Cologne Delhi Melbourne

Hippo Stays Awake

It was a very hot day in the jungle.

"It's too warm to do anything except snooze," thought Hatty Hippo, and she lay down by the waterhole.

Suddenly, the ground began to shake. *Thud, thud, thud!*

"It's only me!" trumpeted Effie Elephant. "I've just come for a quick shower to cool myself down."

Effie stood in the waterhole and sprayed water all over her back. *Slop! Slosh!*

The air was suddenly filled with loud cries.

"*Wheeee!*" It was a troupe of monkeys swinging through the trees. "Anyone for a water fight?" they called loudly.

"*Squawk, squawk!* Yes please!" the parrots shrieked.

Splosh! Splash! Whee! Squawk!

Hatty groaned. How would she ever get to sleep now?

"*Quiet!*" yelled Hatty, louder than any of the other animals. All the noise stopped at once.

"Sorry, Hatty," whispered Effie. "You only had to say something." One by one, the animals tiptoed away.

Finally, the jungle was silent. "Aaaahh!" yawned Hatty, settling down. "Now I'm on my own, I'll get a little bit of peace at last!"

Helpful Baby Elephant

"Giraffe, you've lost your patterns in the mud," said Baby Elephant to his friend. "I'll spray you with my trunk."

"Monkey, you look very tired," said Baby Elephant to his friend. "I'll carry you on my back."

"Oh no, Rhino! You've fallen in the river," said Baby Elephant to his friend. "Hold on to my tail. I'll pull you out!"

Soon Baby Elephant needed a rest. He settled down under a tree and closed his eyes. But no sooner had he closed them than he noticed lots of funny noises. Rustlings and warblings and the distant roar of lions. What if a lion was coming to eat him? Baby Elephant was scared! He opened his eyes with a start.

"What's the matter, Baby Elephant?" asked Monkey.

"When I close my eyes, I start to notice lots of noises," explained Baby Elephant. "It makes me scared to go to sleep. What if a lion ate me while I was asleep?"

"Don't worry, Baby Elephant!" said Monkey. "Now it's our turn to help you. Settle down and close your eyes. Your friends will keep you as safe as safe can be while you rest."

"Thank you!" said Baby Elephant.

Elsie Elephant's Jungle Shower

There wasn't a cloud in the sky, and Elsie Elephant was feeling very hot.

"It's even hot in the shade," she grumbled. "I think I'll go to the river to cool off!"

Tommy Monkey was swinging high up in the tree-tops. "I'm going swimming," Elsie told him. "You can come too, if you like."

"You've got a very long trunk," said Tommy as they wandered towards the river. "What's it for?"

Elsie thought for a minute. "I'm not really sure," she said.

At the river they found Leo Lion standing at the edge of the water, looking in.

"Are you coming for a swim?" asked Elsie.

"Big cats don't swim," sighed Leo. "But I'm so hot!" He watched as Elsie and Tommy splashed into the river.

Elsie saw how hot Leo looked. She looked at her trunk – and had an idea! Filling her trunk with water, she sprayed it all over Leo.

"Thanks, Elsie. This is great!" said Leo.

"Now I know what my long trunk is for!" laughed Elsie.

The Big Blue Egg

One morning, Little Brown Hen found a strange thing in the farmyard. It was big, blue and round. Little Brown Hen walked slowly round the big blue thing. She sniffed it, tapped it with her beak, and listened.

"Well, it's round like an egg," she said. "So it must be an egg. I'll keep it warm until it hatches."

Little Brown Hen settled down to wait for the egg to hatch. She waited… and waited… and waited… but nothing happened.

"Perhaps it isn't warm enough," she worried, giving the egg a nudge with her beak. Oops! The big blue egg toppled out of the nest and began to bounce away.

Boing! Boing! Boing! The egg bounced across the farmyard. "Stop that egg!" cried Little Brown Hen, running after it as fast as she could.

Up jumped Sheeba the sheepdog. She caught the runaway egg between her paws.

"I've been looking for this all day," barked Sheeba. "Thank you for finding it for me!"

"I didn't know that dogs laid eggs!" said Little Brown Hen.

"It's not an egg, silly," laughed Sheeba. "It's my puppy's favourite bouncy ball!"

The Ant and the Grasshopper

Grasshopper was a lively, happy insect, who didn't have a care in the world. He spent the long summer days relaxing in the sunshine or bouncing and dancing through the grass.

"Why are you working so hard?" asked Grasshopper one day, when he saw Ant struggling to carry some grain on her back. "It's such a sunny day! Come and play!"

"I've got no time, Grasshopper," said Ant. "I have to take this grain back to my nest, so that my family and I have enough food when winter comes. Have you built your nest yet?"

"Nest?" laughed Grasshopper. "Who needs a nest when life in the great outdoors is so wonderful? And there's plenty of food — why should I worry?"

Day after day, Grasshopper played, while Ant worked. Soon the trees began to lose their leaves and the days began to get shorter and cooler. But lazy Grasshopper hardly noticed. He was still too busy enjoying himself.

A few days later, it began to snow. Grasshopper suddenly found himself cold and all alone. He was hungry and there wasn't a crumb of food to be found anywhere!

"I know," said Grasshopper. "Ant will help me." So he set out

to look for Ant's nest. It was safe and warm beneath a rock.

Ant came out to see him. "What do you want?" she asked.

"Please, Ant," said Grasshopper, "have you any food to spare?"

Ant looked at him. "All summer long, while we worked hard to gather food and prepare our nest, what did you do?"

"I played and had fun, of course," said Grasshopper. "That's what summer is for!"

"Well, you were wrong, weren't you," said Ant. "If you play all summer, then you must go hungry all winter."

"Yes," said Grasshopper sadly, as a tiny tear fell from the corner of his eye. "I've learned my lesson now. I just hope it isn't too late!"

Ant's heart softened. "Alright, come on in," she said. "I'll find some food for you."

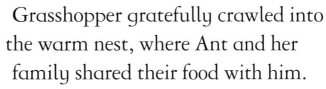

Grasshopper gratefully crawled into the warm nest, where Ant and her family shared their food with him.

By the time spring came around, Grasshopper was fat and fit and ready to start building a nest of his very own!

Copycat Max

Max was a little tiger with a bad habit. He copied everyone! When the parrot said, "Pretty Polly," Max repeated it. Then, when the parrot got cross and said, "Shut up, Max," he repeated that as well. It was very annoying.

One day, Max set off to annoy as many animals as possible.

Soon he met a brown chameleon sitting on a green leaf. The chameleon saw Max and changed his colour to green.

"Watch this then," said Max, and he rolled over and over in some mud. "Now I'm brown," he said.

"You're not really brown," said the chameleon. "Only chameleons can change colour."

"Hmmm!" said Max, annoyed. He rolled in some white feathers. They stuck to the mud. "Look," he said, "now I'm white!"

The chameleon started to laugh. "It won't last," he said.

When Max got home his mother was very angry with him for getting so dirty. She held Max down with her big paw and licked him until he was clean again. It took *ages*. Max wriggled and complained but he couldn't get away.

"It serves you right for being such a copycat," said his mother. "I hope you've learnt your lesson not to do it again."

"Oh, all right," said Max. And, for the moment, he meant it!

Super Snakes

One day Seymour Snake's cousin, Sadie, came to stay.

"Sadie!" cried Seymour. "It's so good to see you! Come and meet my friends! You can play games with us, and –"

"Oh, I don't play games any more," Sadie interrupted. "I've been going to Madame Sylvia's Snake School. Madame Sylvia always says, 'A well-behaved snake may slither and glide and wriggle and slide, but we *don't* swing or sway, or climb or play!'"

"Well, will you come and meet my friends?" Seymour asked.

"Oh, yesss," hissed Sadie. "It would be rude not to!"

"Hey, Seymour!" shouted Maxine Monkey. "Come and play Coconut Catch with Mickey and me!"

"You can come and play, too," Seymour said to Sadie.

"No, thank you," said Sadie. "I'll just watch."

Seymour spent hours hanging and swinging and climbing. Each time, Seymour invited Sadie to join him. But Sadie always said, "I mustn't swing or sway, or climb or play."

Suddenly, Seymour had an idea.

The next day, Sadie was gliding through the jungle when she found Ellen and Emma Elephant, staring up into a tree.

"What's going on?" Sadie asked.

"We were playing Fling the Melon," said Ellen, "and the melon got stuck in that tree. We can't reach it!"

"Oh, dear," said Sadie. "I'm sure Seymour will be happy to climb up and get it for you."

But Seymour had disappeared!

"Can't you help us, Sadie?" Emma asked. "We know about Madame Sylvia's rules. But surely Madame Sylvia must have taught you that it's important to help others."

"Yes, she did," said Sadie. So up she went, winding her way up the trunk and into the branches. She found the melon and gave it a shove. It fell down into Ellen's waiting trunk.

"Thanks, Sadie!" said Emma. "Are you coming down now?"

"Er, not just yet," said Sadie. "I just want to try something first." With a quick wriggle, Sadie coiled herself round the branch and hung upside down above the elephants.

"This is *sssstupendous!*" Sadie hissed. She swung herself over to another tree. "*Wheee!*" she cried.

"I knew you'd like swinging and climbing if you gave it a try," called Seymour, coming out from where he'd been hiding.

"Come up here, Seymour!" Sadie called.

"But what will you tell Madame Sylvia?" asked Seymour.

"I'll just tell her," said Sadie, "that we *must* climb and play, and swing and sway – *all day!*"

Lion's Birthday

It was Lion's birthday.

"Hello, Elephant! Hello, Parrot!" said Lion.

"Er, hello!" trumpeted Elephant. They were both carrying bunches of flowers. "Sorry, Lion. We're kind of busy right now."

"Hello, Giraffe! Hello, Monkey!" said Lion. They were collecting coconuts from a tall palm tree.

"We're too busy to talk!" said Giraffe over his shoulder.

"Hello, Zebra! Hello, Hippo!" said Lion.

Zebra muttered something to Hippo. They disappeared behind a pineapple tree without even saying hello!

"The animals have all forgotten my birthday," said Lion, sadly. He walked slowly through the jungle, feeling very sad.

Then... "*Happy birthday, Lion!*" called all the animals.

"What a *surprise!*" roared Lion happily.

Jed's First Day

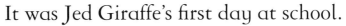

It was Jed Giraffe's first day at school.

"I am too small to go to school, Mum," he said on the way there.

"You're not too small, Jed," said Mum. "Everyone goes to school when they are your age."

"Hello, Jed," said Mrs Beak, the teacher, when they arrived at school.

"I am too small to go to school, Mrs Beak," said Jed.

"Why don't you just go inside and have a look?" said Mrs Beak. "There are lots of other animals here."

But when Jed tried to go into the school he walked into the door. Bump!

"You are certainly not too small, Jed!" said Mrs Beak. "You are too tall! We will have to have school outside," she said.

All the other animals came outside.

"This is Jed," said Mrs Beak.

"Hello, Jed!" they said.

"Hello," said Jed. They looked very friendly.

"We're glad you are here, Jed," said the animals. "School is much more fun outside."

Sad Monkey

Tiny Monkey was sad because he didn't know how to climb.

"All the other monkeys can climb," he thought.

"I'll teach you, Tiny Monkey," said Big Monkey, scampering up a tree. "Cling with your feet, and swing your tail – like this!"

"I'll lift you up into the tree to get you going," said Giraffe.

"I'll catch you if you fall down," said Lion.

"See if you can get all the way up to the top!" said Parrot, fluttering up to the topmost branch in a flash of colour and then flying back down again.

Taking a deep breath, Tiny Monkey climbed onto Giraffe's neck. Her neck swayed as she lifted him high into the tree. Tiny Monkey took a deep breath and swung into the tree.

He clung with his feet and swung with his tail, just as Big Monkey had told him. And it worked! He scampered all the way to the top!

"Look at me! I'm the best climbing monkey in the forest!" he called.

Hide-and-seek

It was playtime at school. The animals were playing hide-and-seek. Lucy Lion counted to ten. The animals ran to hide.

"Ninety-nine… One hundred! I'm coming!" called Lucy.

Lucy looked high and low. She couldn't find Helga Hippo. Lucy looked high and low. She couldn't find Mikey Monkey. Lucy looked high and low. She couldn't find Jed Giraffe.

"Where is everybody?" Lucy wondered. She kept looking. She looked and looked and looked until she started to get tired.

When the bell rang for the end of playtime the animals came out of their hiding places.

"Where's Lucy?" asked Mrs Beak, the teacher.

They looked high and low for Lucy. Helga Hippo couldn't find her. Mikey Monkey couldn't find her. Jed Giraffe couldn't find her.

Then Mrs Beak found her. Lucy had given up. She was fast asleep under a tree!

The Butterfly's Ball

Come take up your hats, and away let us haste
To the butterfly's ball, and the grasshopper's feast.
The trumpeter gadfly has summoned the crew,
And the revels are now only waiting for you.

On the smooth-shaven grass by the side of a wood,
Beneath a broad oak that for ages has stood,
See the children of earth, and the tenants of air,
For an evening's amusement together repair.

And there came the moth, with his plumage of down,
And the hornet in jacket of yellow and brown;
Who with him the wasp, his companion, did bring,
But they promised, that evening, to lay by their sting.

With step so majestic the snail did advance,
And promised the gazers a minuet to dance.
But they all laughed so loud that he pull'd in his head,
And went in his own little chamber to bed.

Then, as evening gave way to the shadows of night,
Their watchman, the glow-worm, came out with a light.
Then home let us hasten, while yet we can see,
For no watchman is waiting for you and for me.

The Lost Valley

Deep in the steamy jungle there was a secret valley that had lain undisturbed since life on Earth began.

A few local people knew about the valley, but they kept well away. You see, stories had been told that terrifying beasts prowled through the lush forests. And it was true – something terrifying did lurk in that valley. For in it lived the last Diplodocus dinosaurs in the world.

One day, a circus owner called Terrible Tony heard about the valley, while tracking down magnificent wild animals for his travelling circus.

"With any luck," he thought, his eyes glinting wickedly, "the monster will be some kind of dangerous animal that will earn me lots of money!" He was determined to find the valley.

Tony armed himself with stun guns, giant nets and even a lasso. He stocked up with provisions and set sail down the river in an inflatable raft.

The further Tony travelled into the jungle, the wilder it became.

One morning, the ground began to shudder. The trees parted and a giant creature burst out of the jungle. It was as long as a town square.

If Tony had had any sense, he would have run for his life. Instead he yelled, "Over here!"

The Diplodocus couldn't hear him. Tony's shouts sounded like tiny, faraway squeaks. However, it had spotted the bright orange raft and made straight for it.

Tony fired a round of darts from his stun gun at the huge creature and waited for it to keel over.

The Diplodocus just shook itself lazily and looked a little bit annoyed. It studied the tiny red-faced man that was irritating it, then bent down and seized Tony in its mouth.

But the Diplodocus, being a plant-eater, didn't eat Tony. Instead, it tossed him away. Then it picked up the raft and hurled it after him.

Tony flew out of the valley and over the hills beyond.

Luckily for him, he landed safely, with an almighty splash, in a distant lagoon.

A few moments later, his raft hit the water right beside him. Tony paddled across that lagoon to the town on its banks as fast as he could go. Then he hailed a taxi to the airport, boarded a plane and never, ever went back to the valley.

Meeting the Diplodocus changed Tony forever. He shut down his circus and released all the animals safely back into the wild.

And the herd of Diplodocus lived happily ever after.

Sleepy Baby Tiger

Baby Tiger yawned as he followed Mum. It was so hot!

"Keep up!" said Mum to the tiger cubs. "Today we are learning how to use our stripes as camouflage."

Baby Tiger wasn't too sure what camouflage was. And the long grass looked so soft and shady. When Mum wasn't looking, he stepped off the trail, curled up and fell fast asleep.

Baby Tiger was woken a little while later by voices.

"He must be somewhere round here," said Mum's voice.

Baby Tiger felt very guilty. "Here I am," he called nervously.

"You were hiding!" said Mum.

"Camouflaged!" said one of the other cubs. "In the long grass."

"Er... yes," said Baby Tiger uncertainly.

Mum nuzzled Baby Tiger. "Don't hide for that long again," she said. "But that was brilliant camouflage. You used your stripes to hide yourself in the long grass like a grown-up tiger."

Baby Tiger smiled.

"Now follow me!" said Mum. "The next lesson is about how to stalk silently through the trees."

Lost Bananas

One day, Elephant was stomping through the jungle when she found a huge bunch of bananas lying under a tree. "Someone must have lost these," she thought. "I'll go and ask Snake."

Elephant found Snake sunbathing on a rock. "Have you lost these bananas, Snake?" asked Elephant.

"How delicioussss! But they're not my bananassss!" hissed Snake, and slithered into the trees.

"I'll just leave them here, then," said Elephant. "Someone will find them." And she plodded back into the jungle.

A giraffe with a long, thin neck came swaying past, and spotted the bananas sitting on the rock.

"What a pity! Someone has lost their dinner," she said, bending down to eat the thick jungle grass.

"Someone must want those bananas!" said Parrot, watching from a tree.

Suddenly she heard a rustling in the branches…

… and lots of monkeys came swinging through the trees!

"Of course! Monkeys love eating bananas!" cried Parrot.

"Wow, what a fantastic bunch of bananas!" said the monkeys. "Let's have a *huge* jungle feast! Come on everybody! Let's eat!"

Sports Day

It was Sports Day at school. First there was the running race. All the animals lined up.

"On your marks, get set, GO!" said Mrs Beak, the teacher. Jed Giraffe had long legs. He won the running race.

Next was a beanbag race. Lucy Lion kept her head very still. She won the beanbag race.

Then there was a hopping race. Mikey Monkey won the hopping race.

But poor Helga Hippo didn't win a single race.

That playtime Helga sat on her own, feeling sorry for herself. "I'm no good at anything," she thought.

Then she heard loud shouts from the pond. Mikey had slipped in!

"Help!" he called. "I can't swim!"

"I can't swim, either!" said Jed.

"I can't swim either!" said Lucy.

"Help!" cried Mikey, desperately.

Helga could swim. She jumped in and saved Mikey. "I might not be a fast runner, a good beanbag balancer or a great hopper," she said. "But I can swim!"

"Well done, Helga!" said Mrs Beak.

A Tiger for Tara

It was Saturday morning. Tara was very excited. She was going to the pet shop to buy a pet.

"What pet shall we buy?" asked Mum, on the way to the pet shop.

"Let's buy a hippo," said Tara.

"Oh, no," said Mum. "A hippo is too fat."

"Let's buy an elephant," said Tara.

"Oh, no," said Mum. "An elephant is too big."

"Let's buy a snake," said Tara.

"Oh, no," said Mum. "A snake is too long and wiggly."

Outside the pet shop was a boy with a toy tiger. "I definitely want to buy a tiger," said Tara. "A tiger would be the best pet."

Inside the pet shop there were big pets and small pets, fat pets and thin pets. But there were no tigers at all.

"These pets are good," said Tara. "But a tiger would be better."

"We can't have a tiger," said Mum. "They are too fierce."

"Wait here," said the pet shop owner. He went into the back room and came back out with a basket of kittens. There were black and white kittens and one small stripy kitten.

"This kitten's name is Tiger," said the owner. "Would you like him as a pet?"

"Oh yes!" said Tara. She gave Tiger a hug. "Tiger is the best pet of all."

Gym Giraffe

Jeremy Giraffe loved going out with his dad to gather juicy green leaves for dinner.

"Remember – the tallest trees have the tastiest leaves, and the tiny top leaves are the tenderest!" His dad would say.

One morning Jeremy decided he wanted to gather leaves on his own, but his neck wouldn't stretch high enough. So Jeremy went back home with his neck hanging down in despair.

"Why, Jeremy, whatever is the matter?" asked his mum. When Jeremy told her, she gave his neck a nuzzle.

"You're still growing," she assured him. But Jeremy couldn't wait for his neck to grow. So he headed to the Jungle Gym to do neck lengthening exercises.

Jeremy spent the next few weeks stretching his neck with all sorts of exercises. Finally, he felt ready to reach for the highest leaves.

Next time Jeremy and his dad went out leaf gathering, Jeremy spotted some juicy leaves at the top of a very tall tree.

"I'm getting those," he said.

"They're so high up!" said Dad. But sure enough, after a big, big stretch, Jeremy reached up and ate them up!

Monkey Mayhem

Mickey, Mandy and Maxine Monkey had finished their breakfast of Mango Munch. Now they were rushing off to play.

"Be careful!" called their mum. "And DON'T make too much noise!"

"We won't!" the three mischievous monkeys promised, leaping across to the next tree. The noise echoed through the whole jungle – Mickey, Mandy and Maxine just didn't know how to be quiet!

Mickey landed on a branch. Maxine and Mandy landed beside him. Just then the branch snapped in two and they shrieked, as they went tumbling down, down, down.

The jungle shook as the three monkeys crashed to the ground, then sprang to their feet.

"Yippee!" the monkeys cheered, brushing themselves off.

The three monkeys then scrambled back up to the top of the trees. They screeched and screamed as they swung through the branches back towards home.

All through the jungle, the animals covered their ears. Nobody would ever keep these three noisy monkeys quiet!

Tiger Footprints

It was a very hot day in the jungle. Tiggy and Mac were playing near the waterfall.

"Wheee!" shouted Tiggy, as she slid on the wet rocks.

Mac was watching a funny-looking frog. It croaked loudly and then hopped away.

"Where are you going?" asked Mac.

When the little frog didn't answer, Mac ran after it.

"Wait for me!" cried Tiggy.

The twins chased the frog through the leafy jungle.

"Look!" shouted Mac suddenly.

Tiggy tumbled to a stop behind him. In front of them sat a whole family of funny-looking frogs.

"The little frog was hopping back home," said Mac.

Tiggy was tired after their long chase. "I want to go home," she groaned.

Mac looked around. They had never been here before. He didn't know how to get home.

"I wish Mum were here," sighed Mac. "She always knows the way home."

As the two cubs looked around, Tiggy noticed a trail of footprints on the soft jungle floor. The footprints were round –

and very big.

"Maybe they'll lead us home," said Mac.

The little tigers followed them carefully, and at the end, they came across a baby elephant.

"This isn't home," said Tiggy. And the two cubs ran away as fast as their little legs could carry them. Finally, the little tigers had run far enough and they stopped for a rest.

"Look! We've made a trail, too," said Mac.

The pair looked back at the footprints that followed them.

"Let's make some more," cried Tiggy. And they ran faster and faster, making a zigzagging trail of tiger footprints.

Then Tiggy noticed some more footprints nearby.

"Those look just like ours," she said, "but much bigger."

"Mum!" they both shouted together.

And the little cubs began to follow the big tiger footprints back through the leafy jungle to where...

... Mum stood waiting.

"Come on, you two little tigers," she said, smiling at her cubs. "Time to go home!"